In memory of

רבקה בת ישראל יעקב ע״ה

Mrs. Ruth Glaser

To whom Jewish education
was of the utmost importance

Her children and Grandchildren
Eli and Yitty Glaser
Avigdor
Sruli
Shmuli
Atara

In Loving Memory of

אסתר מלכה בת הר׳ יואל ע״ה
Esther Shulman

דוב בער בן ר׳ יצחק אייזיק שולמאן ע״ה
Bernard Shulman

חיים יהושע בן דוב בער שולמאן ע״ה
Herbert J. Shulman

יצחק אייזיק בן דוב בער שולמאן ע״ה
Dr. Irving Shulman

יחזקאל בן ר׳ שלום אהרן הכהן ע״ה
Charles Kaplan

אלתר ברכה בת יצחק יוסף ע״ה
Bertha Kaplan

Arthur and Marilyn Shulman and Family
Bayonne, New Jersey

In honor of

Rachel Sopher

and

In loving memory of

Rose and Benjamin Trebach ע״ה

and

Samuel Sopher ע״ה

Marilyn and Morris B. Sopher

In loving memory of

a dear wife, mother,

and grandmother

שרה רחל בת ר׳ מנשה ע״ה

Sarah Rae Brovender

Isidore Brovender
Monsey, New York

Mordechai and Shoshana Summer and Family
Monsey, New York

Chaim and Miriam Brovender and Family
Jerusalem, Israel

In loving memory of

משה בן הרב יואל ע״ה

Morris Summer

חאשקע בת אלחנן שמחה ע״ה

Anna Summer

Mordechai and Shoshana Summer and Family
Monsey, New York

Sally Goldberg and Family
Brooklyn, New York

This book belongs to:

The ArtScroll Children's Holiday Series

Yaffa Ganz

SUCCOS

WITH BINA, BENNY AND CHAGGAI HAYONAH

Illustrated by Liat Benyaminy Ariel

halom! I'm Chaggai the Holiday Dove and you're just in time for one of the happiest times of the year — the holiday of Succos!

Succos is a week of rejoicing, a week of *mitzvos,* a week under the stars in a new and different kind of house. A week when you feel just as though you were in the *Beis Hamikdash!*

Succos begins on the fifteenth of Tishrei, five days after Yom Kippur. It is the third of the *Shalosh Regalim* — the Three Festivals when the Jews came to the *Beis Hamikdash* in Jerusalem. It's a busy time — as full of *mitzvos* as a pomegranate is full of seeds! So get your *lulav* and *esrog* ready, the most joyous week of the year is about to begin.

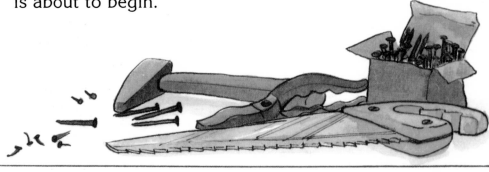

Did you ever "build" a *mitzvah?* If you didn't, Bina and Benny and I are building one right now and you're welcome to watch.

"Oy! After all that work, it's crooked!" Benny bent his head and looked at the *succah.*

"It's not so bad," said Bina. "It justs tilts a tiny bit to one side. When Abba puts the *s'chach* on the top, no one will even notice."

But Benny was still worried. "What if it falls down? I wouldn't want a tumbledown *succah.* It has to stand for seven days. The Jews in the desert never had a crooked *succah,* did they, Chaggai?"

"I wasn't there, of course," said the dove, "but I don't think so. *Hashem* built their *succos* for them."

"He did?! Then I bet they were really special! "

"I'm sure they were," Chaggai agreed, "but the Jews deserved something special. They left their homes in Egypt and followed Moshe into a frightful, dangerous desert!

"*Hashem* gave them new homes to live in — a different kind of home. He gave them *succos*. Some of our rabbis say the *succos* were real huts, made of wood or branches or material. Others say they were made of clouds! *Hashem* changed the shape of the *Ananei Hakavod* — the pillar of clouds which moved before the people — and turned them into small booths. That's why the Torah tells us:

> You shall sit in *succos* for seven days . . . so that your children will know that I placed the Children of Israel in huts when I took them out of the land of Egypt . . . I am *Hashem,* your G-d.

"Those must have been wonderful *succos,*" said Benny wistfully. "I wish I could have seen them."

"I think ours is wonderful too!" said Bina. "And wait until you see the decorations I made in school. It's a *mitzvah* to make the *succah* beautiful."

"Before we put up the decorations, we have to help Abba put on the *s'chach*. It's not a *succah* until it has a roof of *s'chach*. Here comes Abba now!"

"Is it O.K.?" called Benny from on top of the *succah.*

"It's fine!" answered Abba. "There's more shade than sunlight inside, but we can still see the sky. It's almost as if our *succah* were inside a leafy, green cloud!"

"Doesn't the *s'chach* smell nice?" asked Bina. "I love evergreen *s'chach* best of all. There are so many *mitzvos* on Succos using things which grow — the *lulav*, the *esrog*, the *haddasim*, the *aravos*, and the *s'chach*. I wonder why."

"Perhaps because Succos is *Chag Ha'asif.* It's the holiday which comes after the harvest, after we've gathered in all the crops which grew in the fields and stored them for the coming winter," said Abba.

"Did I hang that bird up straight? Doesn't it look a little like Chaggai?" Bina giggled. "Isn't everything lovely?"

"It really is, Bina. You did a great decorating job. Brrr . . . it's getting chilly out here!" Benny buttoned his sweater. "It's too bad Succos couldn't be in the spring or the summer."

"No it's not!" insisted Bina. "Everybody sits outside in the spring or summer, but only Jews move outdoors in the fall."

"Indeed they do," said Abba. "Just when you'd expect them to be celebrating the harvest inside their nice, warm houses, they move out to the *succah*. But *Hashem* takes care of us outside just as well as inside! And now that the *succah* is ready, we'll take care of the next *mitzvah* on our list . . . the *Arba'ah Minim!* Are you ready? Then let's go!"

How lucky Bina and Benny are! Seven *mitzvah*-days to eat and drink and learn and visit and live in the *succah*! Some people even sleep in their *succah*. Of course if it's really cold or rainy, or if you are sick, you can go into the house. But we birds are used to being outside. Maybe I should build my own *succah*. I do have some experience building nests. . .

nd on the first day you shall take for yourselves the fruit of a beautiful tree, a palm branch, myrtle branches, and willows of the brook; and you shall rejoice before *Hashem*, your G-d, for seven days *(Vayikra 23:40)*.

"I know the names of all four *minim*," said Bina proudly. "The fruit of a beautiful tree is the *esrog*. The palm branch is the *lulav*. The myrtle is the *haddas*, and the willow is the *aravah*!"

"And I know that the *esrog* is like the *tzaddik* who learns Torah and does good deeds, because the *esrog* tastes good and has a good smell. The dates of the palm tree — the *lulav* — taste good too, but they have no smell, so the *lulav* is like a Jew who learns Torah but doesn't do any good deeds."

"What about the *haddasim* and the *aravos*?" asked Chaggai.

"The *haddasim* smell good, but they have no taste," said Benny. "So they're like a person who hasn't learned much Torah, but who does *mitzvos*."

"And the *aravos* have no taste and no smell," said Bina. "They're like Jews who have no Torah and no *mitzvos*."

"But all Jews are still one people, which is one of the reasons we hold all four *minim* together when we make the *berachah*," said Chaggai.

"And after the *berachah*," said Bina, "we wave the *lulav* and *esrog* in all six directions — east, south, west, north, up and down — to ask *Hashem* is to protect us from any evil, from whichever direction it comes."

I'd better be careful not to get in the way once they start all that waving . . . those pointy *lulavim* can be dangerous for a dove!

Their father smiled. "What wise children I have today! Perhaps they can also help me find a kosher *esrog*. An *esrog* with no marks or spots; a nice bumpy *esrog*; an *esrog* shaped like a tower, broad at the bottom and narrower towards the top. An especially beautiful *esrog* full of *hiddur mitzvah*."

"And a fresh, green *lulav* — tightly closed, straight like a rod, with a pointy top!" said Benny.

"Don't forget the *haddasim* — moist and green with leaves growing in threes along the stem," said Bina. "And *aravos,* which grow better near a river!"

They looked and searched and examined until finally, they found four perfect *minim*. Bina watched as her father carefully wrapped the *esrog* in soft, silky flax.

"I love the smell of the *esrog*," she said. "It's the smell of Succos!"

"Maybe you love the *esrog* because it's shaped like a heart!" Benny laughed.

"Yes, it is," said Father. "All four *minim* are shaped like parts of the body. Look. The *lulav* is like a spine. The leaves on the *haddasim* are like eyes, and the *aravos* have leaves shaped like a mouth. The *Arba'ah Minim* are a week-long *mitzvah* we do with all our heart and body and soul! But remember," he continued, "it's not a Shabbos *mitzvah*. Shabbos is the one day during Succos when we do not use the *lulav* and *esrog*."

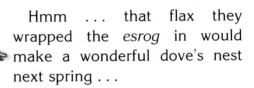

Hmm ... that flax they wrapped the *esrog* in would make a wonderful dove's nest next spring . . .

Baruch atah . . .
asher kideshanu
b'mitzvosav vetzivanu
al mitzvas lulav.

Baruch atah . . .
shehecheyanu
vekeyimanu vehigianu
lazeman hazeh.

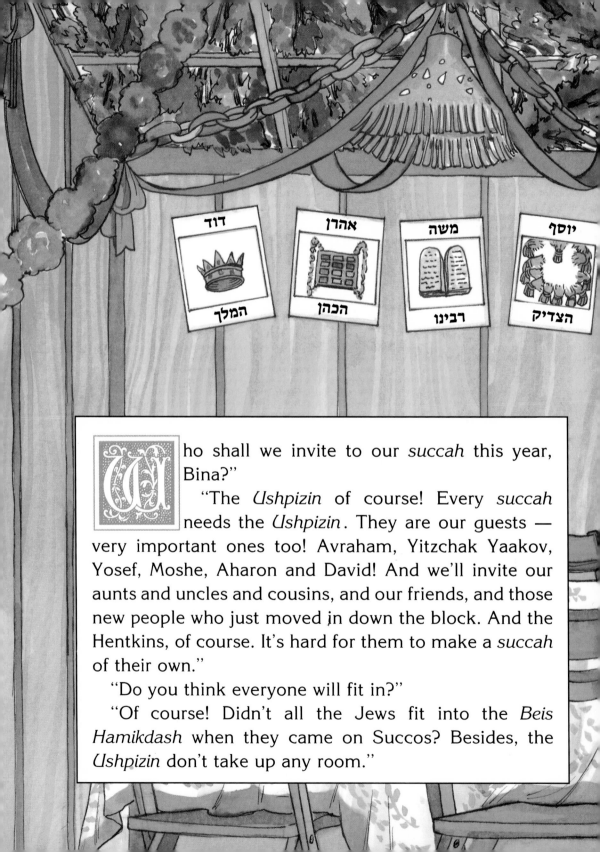

דוד
המלך

אהרן
הכהן

משה
רבינו

יוסף
הצדיק

ho shall we invite to our *succah* this year, Bina?"

"The *Ushpizin* of course! Every *succah* needs the *Ushpizin*. They are our guests — very important ones too! Avraham, Yitzchak Yaakov, Yosef, Moshe, Aharon and David! And we'll invite our aunts and uncles and cousins, and our friends, and those new people who just moved in down the block. And the Hentkins, of course. It's hard for them to make a *succah* of their own."

"Do you think everyone will fit in?"

"Of course! Didn't all the Jews fit into the *Beis Hamikdash* when they came on Succos? Besides, the *Ushpizin* don't take up any room."

"VESAMACHTA BECHAGECHA —
You shall rejoice on your holiday!"

uccos is a time of *simchah* — of joy — and oh my, what rejoicing there was in the *Beis Hamikdash* on Succos! Especially during the *Simchas Beis Hashoeyvah* — the Celebration of Drawing the Water.

Water is a blessing. No one can live without water. Therefore, on Succos (which is the beginning of the rainy season in the Land of Israel) we ask *Hashem* to send enough rain and water for the entire world.

Each evening during Chol Hamoed Succos, a great celebration was held in the Temple. Tens of thousands of people came. The golden lamps were lit. The *Leviim* sang and played their harps and lyres and cymbals. The people danced all night long holding torches and singing songs of praise to *Hashem*. All of Jerusalem rejoiced.

Then, just as the roosters began to crow and announce the beginning of a new day, the people marched out of the *Beis Hamikdash* and down to the Shiloach, an ancient spring of water outside the walls of the city. They drew up pitchers of cold, pure water from the spring and brought them back to the Temple. They prayed the morning prayers, brought the daily offering, and then poured the water from the Shiloach on the *mizbeach* — the altar in the *Beis Hamikdash*.

They ate, drank, studied, rejoiced and prayed again. And in the evening, they lit the golden lamps and began from the beginning. . .

"Whoever has not seen the joy of the *Simchas Beis Hashoeyvah,*" said the Rabbis, "has never seen joy in his life!"

Although we have no *Beis Hamikdash* today, and even though we do not draw water from the Shiloach, we still celebrate the *Simchas Beis Hashoeyvah* each night of Chol Hamoed Succos. We still dance and sing and rejoice with *Hashem*. And someday soon, with His help, we will rebuild the *Beis Hamikdash* in Yerushalayim and have a real *Simchas Beis Hashoeyvah* again!

oshana Rabbah is the end of Succos. It is the last day we use the *lulav* and *esrog* and the *succah*.

Hoshana Rabbah is also the "end" of Yom Kippur. On Hoshana Rabbah, *Hashem* puts the final seal of judgment on His Yom Kippur decisions. Many people stay awake the entire night learning Torah or reciting *Tehillim* — Psalms — and praying that this final, last seal for the year will be a good one.

Each morning of Succos, there is a *lulav* and *esrog* "parade" in *shul* as everyone marches once around the *bimah* and the *chazzan* says the *tefillah "Hoshana."*

On Hoshana Rabbah, however, we march around the *bimah* seven times! Then, towards the end of the *tefillos*, each person takes a bundle of five *aravos* tied tightly together and beats them on the ground, just as the people did in the time of the *Beis Hamikdash.*

"I wish Succos weren't over already. I love the *lulav* and *esrog*. I love our *succah*. I wish Succos could last all year long!"

"I don't think it's such a good idea to be in the *succah* when it snows!" said a practical Benny.

"Oh! I didn't think of that," admitted Bina.

"No one wants Succos to end," said Chaggai. "*Hashem* Himself didn't want the Jews to end the *chag*. That's why He gave us Shemini Atzeres!"

hemini Atzeres — the Eighth Day of Coming Together — is a special, separate holiday with its own prayers and *berachos* and *Kiddush*. When you visit a good friend and are enjoying yourself, you don't want to leave and go home, do you? Well, *Hashem* did not want the Jews to leave His *Beis Hamidkash* either. So He gave them an extra, eighth day to remain in Jerusalem and celebrate. Jews who live outside the Land of Israel still eat in the *succah* on Shemini Atzeres, but the *berachah* for sitting in the *succah* is no longer said.

And no matter where we live, we say *Tefillas Hageshem* — the Prayer for Rain — on Shemini Atzeres. All week long we thought and spoke about water and rain. Now we ask for rains which will be a blessing for the world; rains to nourish the soil, to make the plants and animals grow, to keep the people healthy and strong, to make our planet Earth clean and moist and full of life. From Shemini Atzeres until the holiday of Pesach, three times every day, we will say, *"Mashiv haruach umorid hageshem —* He makes the wind blow and makes the rain descend."

"I know why we only say *mashiv haruach* when the holiday of Succos is over," said Bina. "They didn't want rain to fall before everyone had a chance to leave Jerusalem and return to their homes across the country!"

"And *we* don't want rain to fall when we're sitting in the *succah*!" said Benny.

oday is Simchas Torah — an entire day whose most important *mitzvah* is to rejoice in the Torah! What a wonderful, Jewish day!

The Torah belongs to every Jewish man and woman, boy and girl. It was given to us by G-d and it's ours forever!

There's Benny, over there. He's helping his father carry a *Sefer Torah*. Seven times round, evening and morning, the scrolls will be taken out of the ark and carried around

the *bimah*. Seven circles of dancing and singing; of thanking G-d and rejoicing for the gift of His holy Torah!

There's Bina and her mother. They are very happy. The Torah is theirs too. They keep its *mitzvos* and learn its laws and guard it carefully. They teach it to their children. It is their greatest treasure.

Simchas Torah morning, each man in the *minyan* gets an *aliyah;* he is called to the *bimah* to make the *berachah* before reading from the Torah. Even very young boys are called up to the Torah. They all stand under a *tallis* and make the *berachah* with an older person.

On Simchas Torah, we finish reading *Sefer Devarim,* the last of the Five Books of the Torah. But as soon as we reach the end, we begin reading again from the beginning. Each Shabbos we read one section of the Torah. It will take an entire year to read through all Five Books. And when we finish, we will begin again, and again, and again. The Jewish people are never finished learning and reading the Torah.

The Torah is called our "bride." This year, Bina and Benny's father is the *Chassan Torah* — the Torah's Groom. The *Chassan Torah* is given the *aliyah* when the last part of the Torah is read.

In the Land of Israel, Shemini Atzeres and Simchas Torah are celebrated together on the eighth day.

Sometimes the Torah is called our "bride" and we are called her "groom." Sometimes *we* are called the "bride," and *Hashem* is called the "groom." And sometimes the Jewish people is called "G-d's dove." I like that best of all!

ell, that's it for this year!" Benny looked at the boards of the *succah* neatly piled up and ready to go into the garage. Bina looked at the box of decorations she had carefully packed away. They both looked at their father's *esrog* and *lulav*.

"It's a long time until next Succos, isn't it?" asked Bina.

"I guess so, but there's Chanukah and Tu B'Shvat and Purim and Pesach and Lag Ba'Omer and Shavuos and Rosh Hashanah and Yom Kippur in between," said Benny cheerfully.

"And there's Shabbos every week," added Chaggai. "That's a lot of *simchah* for one year, don't you think?"

"There's *simchah* every day of the year, too! Each day is a time for Torah and *mitzvos* and *simchah*, not just holidays!" said Benny.

"I know," said Bina. "Every day is important and every *chag* is wonderful. But I still think that Succos is the happiest, most wonderful of them all!"

GLOSSARY

Abba — father

arba'ah minim — four species of plants: *lulav, esrog, haddasim,* and *aravos*

Beis Hamikdash — the Holy Temple in Jerusalem

B'ezras Hashem — with G-d's help

bimah — the center platform in the synagogue

chag — holiday

Chag sameach — Have a joyous holiday!

Chol Hamoed — the intermediary days of the holiday

hakafah, hakafos — circuit(s) around the bimah

Hashem — G-d

hiddur mitzvah — the commandment to beautify a mitzvah

Leviim — the Levites who assisted the priests in the Temple in Jerusalem

minim — types, kinds

minyan — a group of ten or more Jewish men or boys over the age of bar mitzvah

mitzvah, mitzvos — commandment, commandments

Moshe — Moses

s'chach — the roof of the *succah;* made of something which grew, but which is no longer connected to the ground, such as branches, leaves, etc.

sefer — book

Shabbos — the Sabbath

shul (Yiddish) — synagogue

succah, succos — booth(s), hut(s) covered with *s'chach* and used during the holiday of Succos

tefillah, tefillos — prayer, prayers

tzaddik — a righteous person

Ushpizin — the seven guests we invite to the *succah*

Yerushalayim — Jerusalem